Nick Ford Mysteries

Alcatraz, The Rock

by
Jerry Stemach

Don Johnston Incorporated
Volo, Illinois

Edited by:

Jerry Stemach, MS, CCC-SLP

AAC Specialist, Adaptive Technology Center, Sonoma County, California

Gail Portnuff Venable, MS, CCC-SLP

Speech-Language Pathologist, Scottish Rite Center for Childhood Language Disorders, San Francisco, California

Dorothy Tyack, MA

Learning Disabilities Specialist, Scottish Rite Center for Childhood Language Disorders, San Francisco, California

Ted S. Hasselbring, PhD

Professor of Special Education, Vanderbilt University, Nashville, Tennessee

Cover Design and Illustration:

Karyl Shields, Jack Nichols

Interior Illustrations:

Phillip Dizick

The Don Johnston logo and Start-to-Finish are trademarks of Don Johnston Incorporated. All rights reserved. Nike is a registered trademark of the Nike Corporation. Ford and Ford Explorer are registered trademarks of the Ford Motor Company. McDonalds is a registered trademark of McDonald's Corporation. Used with permission.

Published by:

Don Johnston Incorporated
26799 West Commerce Drive
DON JOHNSTON **Volo, IL 60073**

International Standard Book Number
ISBN 1-893376-02-8

Contents

**This book is for
Ed Hoch
who left his heart in San Francisco.
Ed wanted everyone to learn how to read.**

Many people have contributed to Alcatraz, The Rock.
My wife, Beverly, and my children, Sarah and Kristie
my friends and colleagues
Ed and Lillian Hoch
Gail Portnuff Venable and Dorothy Tyack
Don Johnston
the entire staff at Don Johnston Incorporated
Ted Hasselbring
Kevin Feldman
Michael Benedetti, Michael Sturgeon, Melia Dicker
Rachel Whitaker, Phillip Dizick
John Palacek, Ellen Sweeney
Greg Damron,
the United States Department of Parks,
and the good people of San Francisco.

Chapter 1

The Drowning Man

Do you hear that noise?" asked Jeff. "Is that gunfire?"

"No," said Mandy. "It's firecrackers. Today is Chinese New Year. The noise is coming from Chinatown."

Mandy Ming and Jeff Ford were on a small beach on Alcatraz Island in San Francisco Bay. It was nighttime. Mandy was standing close to Jeff. She felt lucky. She and Jeff were visiting their friend Greg Miller, the park ranger on Alcatraz. For many years, Alcatraz had been a famous prison for gangsters and criminals.

Now the old prison was empty and Alcatraz was a park for visitors.

Mandy looked at the full moon over the Golden Gate Bridge.

"Look over there," said Jeff. He pointed out across the bay. "Do you see someone in the water?" he asked.

Mandy looked. "Yes," she said. "And I think that person is drowning!"

"The speedboat!" yelled Jeff. He and Mandy raced up the rocky cliff. They ran along a small road.

Then they turned and raced down to a small boat dock. They found a big white speedboat tied up to the dock. Mandy looked at it. The name of the boat was painted in dark green letters: ALCATRAZ. Below the name were more words: United States Department of Parks.

Jeff and Mandy jumped into the boat. Jeff turned the key and a powerful motor roared. Mandy untied the ropes and yelled "Go!"

Jeff pushed on the gas. The boat jumped forward fast. A huge searchlight came on behind them. Mandy turned. She could see someone next to the light. Behind the light, she could see the old prison on Alcatraz. She turned back to the front. The boat was slapping against the waves. She yelled again at Jeff. "I don't see him. He went under!" Jeff slowed down a little, and both of them stared hard into the dark water of the bay.

Then Mandy pointed. "There! Over there! I see him!"

Suddenly there was a splash. Jeff turned around. Mandy dove into the cold water.

Jeff shut off the motor and grabbed a white life ring. Mandy came up for air. "I can't see a thing down there. It's too dark. He won't last long, Jeff. The water is freezing."

Jeff looked around. "Look behind you, Mandy." Mandy turned. She saw something white just under the water. She dove and came up again.

"I have him!" she yelled.

Chapter 2

Mystery Man

Jeff threw the life ring out to Mandy.

It was tied to a long coil of rope.

Mandy grabbed the ring with one hand.

With the other hand, she held onto a

limp body. Jeff pulled on the rope and

got them both close to the boat. He

lifted the man into the boat while

Mandy swam to a short ladder at the

back. Inside the boat the man began to

vomit. Mandy got down next to him

and turned him on his side.

Jeff started the boat. "Get blankets,

Mandy. Cover him up. He's full of water

and he's freezing." The motor roared.

Jeff spun the boat around and headed back to Alcatraz. He could see the dock ahead of them. Four people were waiting there. Jeff knew these people very well. There was his sister, Kris. Next to her was their dad, Nick Ford. Then there was Ken Rice, who was Jeff's best friend, and Greg Miller, the park ranger on Alcatraz. Jeff could count on all of them for help. Jeff slowed the boat down and tossed a rope onto the dock. "I've got it," yelled Ken.

Jeff's dad, Nick, jumped into the boat. "Help me out here," said Nick. "This man is bleeding."

"He's been hit on the head," said Greg. Everyone looked. Blood was running down the man's face. He had a bad cut on his forehead. Greg opened a first aid kit and grabbed a cloth. Nick wiped away the blood. Greg held a clean cloth over the cut. Nick taped the cloth around the man's head.

Greg and Ken helped the man back to the Park First Aid Station.

It was nearly midnight now. There was no one else on Alcatraz Island.

Greg, Ken, Mandy, and Kris cleaned the man up. They put dry pants on him. Then they put him into a bed. The man moaned and tried to speak.

"What did he say?" asked Kris.

"He's speaking Chinese," said Mandy. Mandy Ming was Chinese-American. She could speak Chinese too. She went close to the man. He spoke again and then passed out.

"What?" asked Kris. "What did he say?"

Mandy looked up. "He said 'Please, please. No doctor. No jail.' "

Chapter 3

The Secret

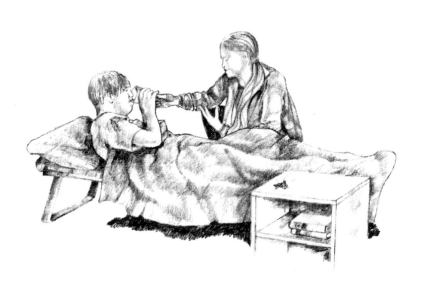

"That man needs a lot of rest," Mandy told the others.

"He has no I.D.," Ken said. "But I found this in his pocket." Ken put a small green stone on the table.

Nick picked it up. "It's carved jade," he said. He looked at it closely. "It looks very old." Nick handed the stone to Mandy. "What is it?" he asked her.

Mandy took the stone. "It's a dragon's head," she said. Dragons are good luck in China. But I never saw one like this. Look here," she said.

"The head of the dragon is broken off at the neck and…"

Mandy stopped. There in the doorway stood the Chinese man. He looked very upset and he was talking very fast. He kept grabbing at his pockets.

Mandy spoke to him. When she showed him the dragon head, he grabbed it away from her.

"That stone must be very important to him," said Jeff.

"We want to help you," said Mandy in Chinese. "But you must help us."

Mandy pointed to a chair. The man sat down. They began to talk.

At last Mandy turned to the others. "This is Quon. Quon Wong. He has come all the way from China on a small fishing boat," she began. "The boat was loaded with illegal fireworks. Quon was working on the boat. The owner of the boat is someone named 'Mr. G.' Mr. G wanted Quon's help to bring the fireworks into America. Quon wanted to sneak into America so he said yes. Quon has a sister here in San Francisco. Her name is Lin Wong."

"But how did he end up in the water?" asked Kris.

Mandy spoke again to Quon. "Quon found a huge shlpment of drugs on the boat. Mr. G was hiding the drugs from him. When Quon found the drugs, Mr. G hit him on the head. Then Mr. G threw Quon off the boat and tried to shoot him."

"We heard the shots," said Jeff.   "Do you remember, Mandy?"

"Now what?" asked Greg.

Ken slapped his hands on the table. "We find Mr. G and bust him," he said.

Chapter 4

Working Vacation

"Hold on," said Greg. "I need to call the police on this one. I could lose my job here. Besides you didn't fly all the way from New York for this. You're here for two reasons. First, you're on vacation. Right?"

Nick nodded and said, "That's right."

Greg spoke again. "Second, I need your help on my project. I'm supposed to build a new Visitors' Center here. But first I have to turn in a report about the plants and animals on Alcatraz Island."

"Right again, Greg," said Nick. "And you really do need our help on that. You almost flunked my Biology class. Remember?"

Everyone laughed. Kris winked at Ken. "We came for a third reason, too," she said. "We came here to help Quon Wong."

"Come on, Nick," said Greg. "I can't keep Quon here. It's against the law. He has no I.D. He's sneaking into San Francisco from China. He fell off a boat that was filled with illegal fireworks."

"And drugs," said Jeff. "Don't forget about the drugs."

"What will the police do?" Nick asked Greg. "The police will put Quon in jail. Then they will send him back to China. The police don't bother the Chinese about fireworks during Chinese New Year because fireworks are part of Chinese New Year. The police won't bother Mr. G because Mr. G will hide his drugs."

Ken spoke up. "I'll tell you, Greg. I go lots of places with Nick and my friends here.

Something like this happens every time. So I just go with it."

It was true. Nick was a Biology teacher at City College of New York. He went on many trips around America and he always took Jeff, Kris, Ken and Mandy. Jeff and Ken were roommates at City College. Kris and Mandy were roommates there too. They did everything together.

Nick looked up at Greg. "Give us two days to help Quon. Then we will work on your report. That will still give us time for a vacation."

Everyone looked at Greg.

Greg looked around. "I don't like it but I'm outnumbered," he said.

Mandy turned to Quon. She spoke to him in Chinese. "No doctors, no jail," she said. "We will find your sister, Lin."

Chapter 5

The Plan

The next morning everyone got up early. Greg cooked bacon and eggs and pancakes. Mandy went to wake up Quon, but his room was empty. They looked down the hall. The door into the jail cells was open. Mandy ran down the hall. There stood Quon. He was looking at all the empty jail cells. He was holding onto the bars. He spoke in Chinese. "I am in America. But I am in jail."

Mandy put her arm on his back. "This is an empty jail. You are free here.

No one will hurt you anymore. Now come and eat."

Quon came into the kitchen. Jeff got up and stood next to Quon. Kris looked at them and laughed. Jeff's T-shirt said SAN FRANCISCO, HARD ROCK CAFE. Quon's T-shirt said ALCATRAZ, HARD LUCK CAFE.

Quon looked at the bacon, eggs, and pancakes. Then he spoke to Mandy. Mandy turned to the others. "He wants rice," she said.

Ken Rice stood up and smiled. He looked at Quon.

"If you want rice, then I'm your man," Ken said. "Rice is my name and help is my game."

Nick said, "I have a plan. I'll take Quon and Mandy with me in my plane. We'll look for Mr. G's boat." Nick looked at Jeff, Ken, and Kris. "You three go to Chinatown in San Francisco. Take Quon's jade stone. Snoop around. Ask lots of questions and try to find Quon's sister."

Nick turned to Greg. "You stay here, Greg. We'll take the cell phones and call you at 12 noon and at 3 o'clock."

Mandy told Quon about the plan but Quon sounded upset. "Quon is afraid of Mr. G," said Mandy. "Quon thinks that Mr. G will find Lin and kill her."

Nick shook his head. "No one will hurt your sister," Nick said. "Tell him, Mandy." Mandy spoke to Quon in Chinese.

Nick asked Quon for the green dragon stone. Quon rubbed the stone and handed it to Mandy. He said something to her.

Mandy turned to the others. "Quon's sister broke this dragon 30 years ago. She gave the head to Quon and kept the rest of it for herself. Now Quon wants to put the dragon back together." Everyone was quiet.

Ken was mad. He shook his fist and said, "Mr. G, don't go messing with Quon and don't go messing with me."

Chapter 6

Off and Running

Everyone waited by Greg's boat. Kris was reading a thick phone book.

Jeff went over to her. "What are you doing, girl?" asked Jeff.

Kris looked up. "I'm looking for Lin Wong in the phone book."

Mandy joined Jeff. "Any luck?" asked Mandy.

"Sort of," said Kris. "There must be 2000 'Wongs' in the phone book. The name 'Lin Wong' is in here 5 times and 'L. Wong' is in here 50 times."

Mandy turned and looked at the Golden Gate Bridge. Thick fog was rolling into the bay. "That is total coolness," she said.

"No," said Jeff. "That is total coldness!" Jeff put on his jacket. "Remember Mark Twain? Mark Twain spent a summer in San Francisco. He said that summer in San Francisco can be the coldest winter of your life."

At last Greg came down to the boat. "You forgot these," he said. He handed two cell phones to Jeff.

"You need to call me at noon and three, remember?"

Jeff handed both phones to Kris. "Here, Kris," Jeff teased. "You can have one for each ear."

Greg fired up the boat. First he took Nick, Mandy, and Quon across the bay to the old Crissy Airport. Nick's plane was parked there.

"We'll fly over every boat on the bay," said Nick.

Mandy winked. "I plan to check out every boy on every boat."

Next Greg took Kris, Jeff, and Ken to the dock at Pier 39. The kids jumped out. Greg waved to them and sped off back to Alcatraz.

Ken took out a map of San Francisco from his backpack. "We can catch a cable car near here. It will take us right into Chinatown."

The three walked past fishing boats. Men were standing by stoves and cooking fresh crab. The smell of the crab and fresh baked french bread filled the air. "It smells like dinner," said Jeff.

They walked past the Wax Museum. They looked in the window. They saw four men. The men were made out of wax. They were holding guns. Kris grabbed Ken's arm. "Those men look so real," said Kris. "They give me the creeps." Kris read the sign next to the men. It said, THE BAD BOYS OF ALCATRAZ.

"Mr. G should be in there, too," said Ken. "I want to see that dude locked up behind bars. Then I want to throw away the key."

Chapter 7

The Bad Boys of Alcatraz

Kris and Ken and Jeff stared at the four wax men. "They were the worst gang members of the 1930's," said Jeff.

"That big fat man is Al Capone," said Ken. "He had a gang in Chicago in the 1930's. He made whiskey and sold it for big bucks. Whiskey was against the law then. Al Capone was called Scarface because he had a bad cut across his face. They arrested him and he spent 11 years in Alcatraz. Do you see those two dudes next to him?

That's Creepy Karpis and Machine Gun Kelly."

"And who's that skinny one?" asked Kris.

"That's Frank Morris, the bank robber," said Ken. "He escaped from Alcatraz."

"What?" asked Kris. "I thought that no one ever escaped from Alcatraz."

Ken kept looking at Frank's face. "Frank Morris escaped," said Ken. "He knew lots of tricks.

He used a spoon and a nail clipper and he dug his way out of his cell. He made a mask of his own face and stuck it in his bed. The guards thought Frank was sleeping. But Frank was on his way out."

Kris stopped Ken. "The water in the bay is way too cold. He would drown."

Ken grinned. "Frank had a bunch of raincoats," he said. He glued them together and made a little boat. Then he..."

Just then a bell began to clang. Everyone turned. A cable car was pulling out of the cable car stop. "Kiss that cable car good-bye. We'll never catch it," said Jeff.

"No, let's go for it!" said Ken. The three kids ran down the street. Ken was in the lead. They ran through a red light. They raced up a steep hill. Jeff nearly hit an old lady. Two old men yelled something. Then the men jumped out of the way.

"Jump on!" yelled Ken. Cars were coming down the hill. Brakes squealed.

Ken and Jeff jumped. They grabbed an outside pole on the cable car. Jeff turned. Kris was still ten feet away. Jeff leaned out and reached for Kris.
Kris stretched out her arm. Jeff could feel the tips of her fingers. He grabbed her hand and pulled hard. Kris jumped and landed on the step of the cable car.

Jeff laughed. "Can't you run any faster?" he asked her.

Ken laughed, too. "Get a new pair of shoes, woman. Put some air in your feet. Nike Air."

Chapter 8

The Gang of Five

The three kids got off the cable car at Grant Street in Chinatown. There was a loud boom. Bang! Bang! Bang! Bang! Jeff ducked. Kris jumped back. Ken laughed again. "It's Chinese New Year. Firecrackers! Remember?" he said.

Kris looked around. Bits of red paper were all over the street.

"It's paper from firecrackers," said Ken.

A small Chinese boy came up to them. "You want firecrackers?" he asked. "Dollar a pack. Dollar a pack."

Jeff showed the boy a five dollar bill. "I'll take ten packs," said Jeff.

"I'll sell you eight packs and give you matches for free," said the boy. Jeff shook his head and started to walk away. The boy yelled back at Jeff. "OK, OK, ten packs, five bucks," he said. Jeff paid him.

Jeff handed the packs of firecrackers and matches to Ken and Kris. "Keep these in your pockets," said Jeff. "We may need them." Jeff took out a five dollar bill and held it up to the boy.

"Hey, kid," said Jeff. "Where did you get this stuff?"

The boy shook his head. He said, "Can't say. Can't say."

Jeff held up $20 more. "Can you say for 25 bucks?"

The boy grabbed the money out of Jeff's hand and ran off. Jeff and Ken ran after him. In two blocks, the boy turned into an alley that ended at some trash cans. Jeff and Ken went all the way to the trash cans but they did not see the boy. Jeff and Ken turned to leave.

Suddenly a gang of five Chinese boys stepped out of a doorway and blocked the alley. A big boy was holding a chain. Another boy had a long stick. A third boy held a bat. Jeff and Ken were trapped.

"You must be lost," said the boy with the bat.

Ken held up two packs of firecrackers. Jeff took out some matches and lit both packs at the same time. Then Ken threw the packs of firecrackers at the gang of boys.

The big boy stepped on one pack and picked up the other pack. He squeezed it in his fist. "I eat firecrackers," said the boy. "Thanks for lunch."

"People like you come to the trash cans for one thing," said another boy.

Jeff took a chance. "I know," he said. "Mr. G sent us." Jeff looked at the faces of the boys. The boys looked at each other. Jeff spoke again. "Mr. G said that we could get drugs here. But Mr. G won't be happy. Instead of drugs, you have chains, a stick, and a bat."

"You got cash?" asked the big Chinese boy.

Jeff took out a 100 dollar bill. "I just want a drug sample for now," he said.

The boy next to Jeff grabbed the money. Another boy took out a little bag of white powder. He handed it to Jeff. Jeff said, "We'll try it. Then we'll get back to you." Jeff and Ken turned and walked out of the alley.

Chapter 9

A Dragon in the Window

Kris had been following Jeff and Ken. She met them outside the alley. She had her cell phone with her. "I was ready to call 9-1-1, and you two just walk out."

Jeff spoke. "We got lucky back there."

"Let's get out of here," said Ken. "Those dudes play dirty. And big boy back there likes to eat firecrackers."

The three kids walked fast. Ken looked at his watch. It was 12:30 and they had not called Greg yet. They went into a McDonalds and sat down.

Kris punched in Greg's number. One ring. Two rings. Three rings. Four rings. "Come on, Greg," said Kris. "Pick up the phone."

Back on Alcatraz, Greg was putting gas in his boat. He heard the phone ring and he knew that it was Kris. Greg picked up the phone and said, "You're late."

"I know I'm late," said Kris. "How is Nick?"

"Nick found Mr. G's boat by Pier 44," said Greg. "Tell Ken and Jeff to go down there and check it out.

Nick and Mandy and Quon will meet you in Chinatown at 2 o'clock."

Kris spoke. "OK. Tell Nick to meet me at the McDonalds on Grant Street."

Kris told the boys about the boat. Ken and Jeff took the cell phone and left for Pier 44. Kris walked along Grant Street. "Nick, Mandy, and Quon won't get here till 2 o'clock. I have time to look for Quon's sister," she said to herself. Kris stopped at a store window. It was full of carved jade. Kris felt Quon's stone in her pocket and went inside the store.

"Can I help you?" asked a small Chinese lady in a red silk dress.

Kris handed Quon's jade stone to the lady.

The lady looked at the dragon head. "Very, very old," said the lady. "No good broke. Much money, not broke. You take back. You go now. Go away." She gave the dragon head back to Kris.

"But I want to find the rest of it," said Kris.

"No can help," said the lady.
"Bad luck, bad luck."

Kris left the shop and walked on up
Grant Street. She walked past a
Chinese restaurant. The window was
full of Chinese food for tea lunch. Kris
licked her lips. "Dim Sum," she said.
She looked at the plates of pork buns,
shrimp rolls, and sticky rice. Then she
saw it! In the corner of the window
was a broken jade dragon. Kris looked
at it for a long time.

She looked at Quon's dragon. "It looks like the same stone!" cried Kris. She looked back down the street. Nick, Mandy, and Quon were waiting outside McDonalds.

Chapter 10

Help in Chinatown

Kris took Nick, Mandy, and Quon back to the Dim Sum restaurant. She showed them the broken dragon in the window. "There is a sign next to the dragon," said Kris. "The sign is written in Chinese. What does it say?"

"I can't read Chinese," said Mandy. She asked Quon what it said. "Quon can't read at all," she said. "Quon had to work in China when he was a boy. He never got to go to school."

The four went inside the restaurant. A waitress took them to a table by the window.

"Do you need a menu?" she asked.

"No," said Mandy. "We're having Dim Sum." Mandy spoke to Nick and Kris. "I hope that Quon likes this," said Mandy. "He has never seen this kind of food. In China, he ate one bowl of rice each day. His family shared one fish." Quon looked at all the plates of Dim Sum food. He spoke to Mandy. Mandy smiled. "Quon said people who eat like this must be very rich."

After lunch, Nick spoke. "We better go. I want to check on the boys."

"Wait," said Kris. The waitress brought the bill. Kris handed her the money and the broken dragon head. "I saw one of these in your window," Kris told her.

The waitress looked at Mandy and Quon. "Do you want help with that?" asked the waitress.

"I think so," answered Kris. Quon looked up at the waitress.

"Then come with me," said the waitress. She led them past the kitchen and into a small room. She pulled back a curtain.

Three Chinese women were sitting in front of computers. There was a fax machine. Each woman was talking on a phone.

"What is this?" asked Mandy.

"Help for missing people," answered the waitress. Everyone in Chinatown has family back in China. We help people find their family in China." The waitress spoke to one of the women at a computer. The waitress said, "These people are looking for Lin Wong."

The lady at the computer stared. "Lin Wong?" she asked.

"Yes," said the waitress. "This is her brother, Quon Wong. He wants to find his sister, Lin Wong."

"That just can't be," said the lady. She looked at a paper. "Another man just called here for Lin Wong. They are meeting each other right now."

"Who?" asked the waitress. "Who called?"

"A man," answered the lady at the computer. "His name was Mr. G."

Chapter 11

A Surprise on the Boat

Nick flew into action. "I'll call 9-1-1," he said. He tossed his own cell phone to Mandy. "You call the boys," he said. Nick picked up a phone in the room and hit 9-1-1. "This is Nick Ford. I am with the Park Service from Alcatraz. I want to report a crime. Get me the police, and do it fast."

Ken and Jeff heard their cell phone ring. It was Mandy. Ken spoke softly into the phone. "We are on Mr. G's fishing boat," said Ken. "We are down below the deck.

This boat is filled with fireworks. There
is a big shipment of drugs here, too.
Mr. G is upstairs with that gang of kids.
Some lady is with them."

Mandy spoke to Ken. "It's Lin Wong,
Quon's sister. She has been
kidnapped. Nick has just called the
police. We will get you out of this
somehow," said Mandy.

Just then, the motor on the fishing
boat started up. "Do you hear that?"
asked Ken. "I have a bad feeling about
this," he said to Mandy.

"Nick wants you to stay on the phone," said Mandy. "Keep talking to me. Tell me where you are and what is happening."

"I think Mr. G is taking this boat to Alcatraz," answered Ken. Suddenly, a door above Ken and Jeff opened. A man was coming down the ladder! Ken and Jeff squeezed behind boxes of fireworks and watched. The man opened a big wooden box. It was filled with guns! The man passed the guns up to someone on the deck above.

Next, he passed up plastic bags that were filled with white powder.

"Drugs," thought Ken. The man went up the ladder. The motor on the boat stopped. The boys heard a splash. Voices on the deck were talking in Chinese. Soon it was quiet. Ken could hear the waves splashing against the boat. Jeff climbed the ladder and peeked out. Alcatraz was only 100 yards away. The gang of Chinese boys, Mr. G, and a lady were in a small rowboat going toward Alcatraz.

The floor of the rowboat was filled with guns and the bags of drugs.

Jeff spoke to Ken. "They are going to hide the guns and drugs on Alcatraz," he said. "They will be coming back to the boat for the rest of their stuff."

"There is only one thing we can do," said Ken. "We need to swim to Alcatraz. I'll tell Nick to give us 15 minutes. Then the cops can blow up this fishing boat. Mr. G will be stuck on Alcatraz." Ken told Mandy the plan. Quickly, Mandy told Nick about the plan.

"Nick doesn't like your plan," said Mandy.

Jeff grabbed the phone and spoke into it. "Tell Nick that we don't like the plan either. Just do it."

Chapter 12

Fireworks on Alcatraz

Nick called Greg on Alcatraz and told him the plan. Greg ran to the east end of Alcatraz. He spotted the boys in the water. He saw a police chopper flying toward the fishing boat. The chopper got closer. Greg looked at his watch. In 30 seconds the chopper would blow up the fishing boat. But the boys were still 100 feet away from shore. The chopper fired a gun at the fishing boat. There was a huge explosion. Fireworks and smoke filled the air. Small rockets were shooting out of the burning boat.

Greg looked into the smoke and
tried to see Jeff and Ken. The boys
were gone.

Greg grabbed his cell phone. He hit
9-1-1. "This is Ranger Greg Miller on
Alcatraz. Call the cops. They just had a
chopper here. I need them back here
fast. Get them on the phone with me."

Greg ran for the guard tower on
Alcatraz. "I've got to spot the boys,"
he said.

Greg ran up the stairs of the old
guard tower. He looked far below. He
could see the burning boat.

Fireworks were still exploding. He looked into the water. No Ken. No Jeff. Then Greg saw something bad.

The gang of boys were standing on the rocks by the water. They each held a gun and pointed it at the water. Mr G was there too. Lin was tied up next to him. Mr. G's rowboat was just out of the water on the rocks.

A voice came from Greg's cell phone. "This is Chopper 1, Chopper 1. Do you hear me, Ranger Greg? Come in, Ranger Greg."

Greg grabbed his phone. "I hear you, Chopper 1," he said. "Get that big bird back here fast. I got two kids in the water. And six men are pointing guns at them. "

The man on the chopper spoke. "We'll be there in 30 seconds."

Greg turned. He saw the chopper. Greg reached down and flipped on a switch. He picked up a microphone. He hoped that he could trick Mr. G and the gang into thinking that there were a lot of people there. A big loudspeaker squealed.

Greg spoke into the microphone. "Throw down your guns or I will order my men to shoot. We have you surrounded."

Greg's voice filled the air. The Chinese boys looked around. Then they saw the chopper. It was coming in low and fast. The boys threw down their guns. Mr. G turned and looked up. He aimed his gun at the chopper.

Just then, Ken stood up out of the water. He and Jeff had been hiding behind Mr. G's rowboat. Ken yelled, "Over here!" Mr. G turned.

Now Jeff stood up and hit Mr. G from behind with an oar. Mr. G slipped and fell into the water. The chopper was now just ten feet over their heads. Water sprayed everywhere. Ken and Jeff each grabbed a gun. Then they grabbed Lin.

Chapter 13

One Dragon

Police from San Francisco came to Alcatraz on a police boat. A TV news crew came with them. The police put the Chinese boys and Mr. G in handcuffs.

Ken went up to Mr. G. "Don't you ever get in my face again," said Ken.

A cop grabbed Mr. G by the arm. The cop turned Mr. G around. "You're out of here," said the cop.

Ken called after them. "Don't forget to throw away the key," he yelled.

Greg, Jeff, and Ken took Lin back to the ranger station. They went into the kitchen and sat down. "This has been quite a day," said Greg.

"It's not over yet," said Jeff. He turned to Lin. "Lin," said Jeff. "We are really glad to meet you."

Lin was crying. "You saved me. Those men were going to shoot me."

Ken spoke. "You and Quon are both safe now. You can..."

Lin stopped Ken. She said, "Quon? You know my brother in China?"

Greg smiled and said, "Quon isn't in China anymore. He is here." Just then, Nick, Kris, and Mandy came into the room. Quon came in behind them.

Lin jumped up and ran over to Quon. She threw her arms around him and started to cry again. "Quon, Quon, my little brother," she said in Chinese. "Is it you? I have not seen you for 30 years," she said.

Ken, Jeff, and Greg told Lin all about Quon. They told her about the boat and about Mr. G. They told her about the drugs and guns.

They told her about Quon's broken dragon.

Lin reached into her pocket. She held out her hand toward the boys. Slowly she opened her hand. Everyone looked. They saw the rest of the broken jade dragon.

"There it is," said Jeff. "The dragon has come home."

Kris, Ken, Mandy, and Jeff made a circle around Lin and Quon. Kris felt so happy that she started to cry. "This dragon will never be apart again," she said.

Greg held up his hands. "I am proud of all of you. This story has a happy ending," he said. I will tell the police that Quon has helped us stop a big shipment of drugs. He can start a new life here and the rest of you can start your vacation."

"Not so fast, Greg," said Nick. "First we have to help you with your report about the plants and animals on Alcatraz. You would be lost without us."

Greg smiled. "OK, Nick," he said. "This time I'll do what you say."

The End

A Note from the Start-to-Finish Editors

You will notice that Start-to-Finish Books look different from other high-low readers and chapter books. The text layout of this book coordinates with the other media components (CD and audiocassette) of the Start-to-Finish series.

The text in the book matches, line-for-line and page-for-page, the text shown on the computer screen, enabling readers to follow along easily in the book. Each page ends in a complete sentence so that the student can either practice the page (repeat reading) or turn the page to continue with the story. If the next sentence cannot fit on the page in its entirety, it has been shifted to the next page. For this reason, the sentence at the top of a page may not be indented, signaling that it is part of the paragraph from the preceding page.

Words are not hyphenated at the ends of lines. This sometimes creates extra space at the end of a line, but eliminates confusion for the struggling reader.